KIDS' BEST

I LOVE MY DOG

FIELD GUIDE

TO

Neighborhood Dogs

Written and Illustrated by

Michael J. Rosen

Workman Publishing, New York

Library of Congress Cataloging-in-Publication Data

Rosen, Michael J.
[Kids' best dog book]
Kids' best dog book : Kids' best field guide to neighborhood dogs / written and illustrated by Michael J. Rosen : photographs by Dennis Mosner.
    p. cm.
Includes index.

ISBN 1-56305-317-9 (pbk.)

1. Dogs—Juvenile literature. 2. Dog breeds—Juvenile literature.
[1. Dogs. 2. Dog breeds.] I. Mosner, Dennis, ill. II. Rosen, Michael J., 1954– Kids' best field guide to neighborhood dogs.
1993. III. Title.
SF426.5.R65 1993
636.7′ 1—dc20
92-50930 CIP AC

Front cover photograph by Dennis Mosner Photography.

Workman books are available at special discounts when purchased in bulk for premiums and sales promotions as well as for fundraising or educational use. Special editions or book excerpts can also be created to specification. For details, contact the Special Sales Director at the address below.

Workman Publishing Company, Inc.
708 Broadway
New York, NY 10003

Manufactured in the United States of America
First printing July 1993
10 9 8 7 6 5 4 3 2 1

Contents

This field guide offers you a handy method of identifying almost any dog you're likely to meet in your neighborhood. You'll learn what kind of breed it is, what kind of work it was originally bred to do, how it may behave around you, and some interesting facts about its background.

The dogs recognized by the American Kennel Club are grouped by similar bodies, backgrounds or talents. Those key parts on a dog's body that you'll be likely to notice first—coat color, markings, shape of the ears, kind of tail—have their own names and descriptions. All these features are shown on pages 7–10 and make breed identification easier.

Only the most common breeds are illustrated in this guide. Other dogs that closely resemble these are described on page 18. When you meet a breed of dog not listed here, use one of the fill-in pages at the back of the book to add it to your **life list**— that's a record of all the different kinds of dogs you've seen in your life.

Let's say you're walking down the street and you see a new dog. Take out the guide and begin asking yourself these questions, letting your answers guide you through the book.

What size is the dog? The breeds are grouped by size (see page 11), so unless the dog is a puppy, turn to the appropriate section. Toy dogs come first (look for red bars on the page), followed by miniature dogs (yellow bars), medium dogs (green bars), and then large dogs (blue bars). If you meet a dog that looks just like one in this guide but doesn't match the size, it could be that you've found a miniature or a giant version of a pictured breed. Poodles, Dachshunds, Schnauzers, and several other dogs are bred in more than one size. This symbol (+) means to see page 18 for a list of breeds that vary in size.

Is the dog a puppy? Does it have very large feet or long legs for its body size? Is it showing those unmistakably puppyish behaviors like nipping, scampering around, and acting submissive? If the answer is yes, look in a dog group larger than the puppy's current size.

What is the dog's most noticeable feature? Perhaps the dog in front of you has a thin whip tail or a very thick double coat. Start looking for that feature among the dogs in its size section. (Don't use the dog's color for making your match; nearly every dog comes in a variety of colors.)

Do the other descriptions in that entry fit the dog? If you find a likely match, read the entry to see if it describes the dog. (Remember, many breeds have the same tail type or ear type, so expect several matches for a single trait and choose among them.) If you don't find a match, turn pages until you find another dog with that characteristic, or choose another feature—the dog's coat type, for example—and search the guide for matching dogs.

Once you've made a correct identification, check the box on the bar at the bottom of the section to add that dog to your life list.

It's usually fun to talk to a dog's owner and family members; they're sure to know interesting details about both the breed and the individual dog. Although you'll learn about specific breeds in this guide, if you're considering adopting a purebred dog, you'll need much more information. Talk with local breeders and look for books about the breed you are interested in to make sure that your family and that type of dog would be a good match.

Points, parts, and traits—these are your clues for identifying dogs. **Points** are terms for key places on a dog's body. Two of the dog's most telltale **parts** are the ears and tail. And **traits,** at least the physical ones, are those exceptional features of the dog's coat or coloring that you're sure to notice.

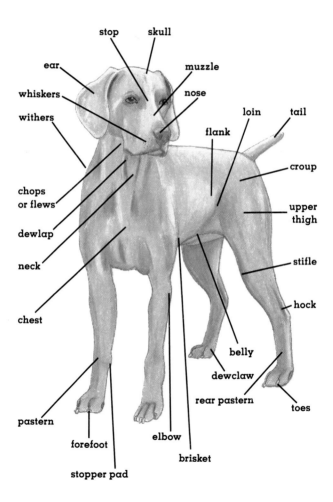

You may see a Basset Hound's long ears swinging and nearly sweeping the floor, a Welsh Corgi's tall ears shifting to catch a sound from another direction, or a Whippet's ears perked into small wings. Here are the names for all the droopy, flappy, tall, and tiny ears you'll see.

Bat ears are broad at the bottom and point straight up as in a Samoyed, Boston Terrier, and Akita.

Rose ears look like small petals and fold over gently, as in a Pug or Bulldog.

Hanging ears are the long, droopy ears on many hounds, setters, retrievers, and poodles.

Prick and tulip ears are curved, tall, and pointed slightly forward; they occur naturally, without surgical cropping, in the German Shepherd, Chow Chow, and in the spitz family. Dobermans, Great Danes, and Schnauzers are among those whose ears are often cropped during puppyhood.

Semi-prick ears are tall also, but bend at the tips, as in the Collie or Whippet.

Button ears have small flaps folded forward against the forehead, as in a Shar Pei, Fox Terrier, or Airedale.

Drop ears are folded and lie flat alongside the head, as in the Border Terrier, Bullmastiff, or Irish Wolfhound.

L ong and plumed, short and wiggly—tail shapes are mostly for balance and for communicating. Here are the basic tails wagging around your block.

Ring tail: a curling tail, set high on the body, that forms a circle over the dog's back (Pekingese, Chow Chow).

Otter tail: a thick, tapered, blunt tail without feathering that hangs down without a curve (Labrador Retriever).

Plume tail: a bushy tail of long fringe that either hangs down or over the back (Pomeranian, Lhasa Apso).

Fringe tail: a long, feathered tail (Golden Retriever, setters).

Brush tail: a thick, bushy tail that resembles a fox's (Rough Collie, Bernese Mountain Dog, Newfoundland).

Bobbed or **docked tail:** a tail that is surgically cut to a specific length shortly after the dog's birth. Many breeders no longer perform this operation.

Pompon: the clipped poodle's trademark tail-end poof.

Screw tail: a small twisted or kinked tail (Pug, Basenji).

Gay tail: a tail that's held high in the air (Beagle, Cairn Terrier).

Whip tail: very long and thin (Manchester Terrier, Bull Terrier, Great Dane, Greyhound).

Some coat colors you'll identify easily: white, brown (also called chocolate or liver), black, tan, gray, red (which usually means a rusty orange color), sable (a brown-orange), gold, and fawn (light brown). Some breeds do come with their own unusual descriptions, such as deadgrass (Chesapeake Bay Retrievers), chestnut (Irish Setters), or apricot (Poodles). Here are a few useful terms.

 Brindle: darker hairs on a lighter background create a loose black striping (Great Danes, American Staffordshire Terriers, Whippets).

 Sable: patches of black-tipped hair on a coat that's silver, gray, tan, or gold (Malamute).

 Tricolor: a coat in any three colors—usually black, brown, and white.

 Particolored: a coat composed in distinct patches of two or more colors.

 Roan: a coat with a mixture of colored and white hairs, that gives a blended color (English Setter or Brittany).

 Grizzled: a bluish-gray coat that's a mixture of bluish-gray, reddish, and black hairs—typical in Old English Sheepdogs.

 Blue merle: a coat that is marbled or spotted with black, blue, and gray hairs, as in an Australian Cattle Dog or a Cardigan Welsh Corgi.

Common patterns and colorings on a dog's coat are also given names. See if you can spot any dogs with these special features.

Ticking: small clusters of black or other dark hairs that appear on a white coat, giving a dotted look.

Saddle: a different color that extends over the dog's back in the shape of a saddle.

Kiss marks: small, colored (often brown) spots around the face.

Blaze: a stripe of white that runs down the forehead, dividing the eyes.

Mask: a clearly defined foreface (around the eyes) of a different color, which may look like goggles or a blindfold.

Feathering: the long fringe that hangs from the dog's belly, tail, legs, or ears.

Trousers: the thick feathering on the hind legs of dogs like the Golden Retriever.

Apron: this same long feathering at the base of the neck and chest on dogs like the Rough Collie.

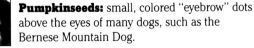

Pumpkinseeds: small, colored "eyebrow" dots above the eyes of many dogs, such as the Bernese Mountain Dog.

Official Sizes

Dogs are divided into four groups according to height, which is measured from the ground to the dog's withers.

- **Toy dogs** are shorter than 9½ inches.

- **Miniature dogs** stand from 9½ to 16 inches tall.

- **Medium dogs** reach from 16 to 24½ inches.

- **Large dogs** are those that rise above 24½ inches at the withers. (The Irish Wolfhound, the tallest breed, averages a height of 33 inches.)

The Seven Dog Groups (Plus One)

In the thousands of years since our two species began to live together, people have bred the dog into an astonishing array of shapes, sizes, and talents. The seven dog groups that follow demonstrate the variety of canines created in the long history of the dog.

Of more than 440 modern dog breeds, the American Kennel Club chooses to recognize over 140 dogs and to divide them into seven different groups according to the kind of work they originally performed. The AKC has also created an eighth group to include a few other popular breeds. Kennel clubs in other countries may recognize different dogs that are more popular in their region.

Think of each group as a separate dog club whose members share common interests, enjoy doing similar things, and behave (somewhat) according to club rules. Although there can be wide variations in size and temperament within each group, this is a good way for you to become familiar with the many dogs you'll meet.

Sporting Dogs

These are the dogs originally bred for bird hunting. Pointers help the hunter by tracking game birds; when they catch the scent of a nearby bird, they freeze and point so that the hunter can move ahead and scare the hiding bird into the air. Many spaniels search for game birds close to the hunter, flushing the bird from the bushes into the air. Retrievers go after the birds a hunter shoots; some are great swimmers and others are rugged runners.

Irish Setter

Hounds

This group contains dogs bred for hunting mammals. Hounds developed along two lines. Long-limbed animals were created for fast long-distance running and sharp vision; these are the gaze- or sighthounds. Medium-size and smaller dogs were bred for their tracking and smelling skills; these are the scent hounds. Specific breeds were trained to hunt badgers, otters, bear, deer, foxes, hares—and even man. (The Bloodhound is often used in tracking lost people.)

American Foxhound

Working Dogs

These dogs were bred for all kinds of work: pulling carts and sleds; guarding lands, homes, or herds; assisting police officers, soldiers, or people with physical difficulties. Each of these dogs—especially the giant breeds—requires plenty of training, patience, exercise, and work opportunities.

Akita

Terriers

The word "terrier" comes from a Latin root word meaning "earth." Included here are more than twenty small, feisty dogs originally bred for pursuing rats and other small creatures underground into their burrows and dens.

At some point in history, terriers were bred with the Bulldog to create fighting dogs. The three larger, broad-chested descendants are found in this group: the Bull, Staffordshire Bull, and American Staffordshire Terriers.

These dogs all possess "terrier fire," an extremely courageous, enthusiastic, and eager personality.

Wire Fox Terrier

Toys

This is a group of dogs bred to be companions—often constant companions. Some dogs live nearly their entire lives in the arms of royalty, while others enjoy the laps, cushions, or beds of their human family. Some are nervous, easily chilled and frightened, but others act as ferocious as a dog fifty times their weight. Except for the Chihuahua, which originated in Mexico, toy dogs are native to other continents.

Shih Tzu

Herding Dogs

These dogs originally worked with farmers and shepherds to move animals from fields and pastures to pens and barns. Some members have great endurance for a long day of herding, while others have thick coats for protection against mountain weather and menacing wolves. These dogs were developed to work closely with humans and, in fact, play a critical part in our own evolution: Their teamwork helped our ancestors change from a wandering, gathering band of hunters into a settled community that could raise and grow its own food.

Old English Sheepdog

Non-Sporting Dogs

This seventh group pulls together dogs that don't quite fit other categories. The non-sporting dogs are the Bichon Frise, Boston and Tibetan terriers, Bulldog and French Bulldog, Standard and Miniature Poodles, Schipperke, Chow Chow, Dalmatian, Keeshond, Lhasa Apso, Chinese Shar Pei, Finnish Spitz, and Tibetan Spaniel.

Dalmatian

Miscellaneous Dogs

Some of the rarer breeds that the AKC doesn't register or include in its competitions are clustered together here in the Miscellaneous Group. This says nothing about the breed's qualities, only that the AKC doesn't feel this country has enough supporters, responsible breeders, and dogs with well-documented ancestry to compete in their shows. Once a "newcomer" breed is finally popular enough, it moves into one of the other seven groups.

Border Collie

Here are the American Kennel Club's member breeds, listed according to their official group. The names appearing in darker type are pictured in this guide, and many other related breeds are described.

Sporting Dogs

American Water Spaniel
Brittany
Chesapeake Bay Retriever
Clumber Spaniel
Cocker Spaniel
Curly-Coated Retriever
English Cocker Spaniel
English Setter
English Springer Spaniel
Field Spaniel
Flat-Coated Retriever
German Shorthaired
    Pointer
German Wirehaired
    Pointer
Golden Retriever
Gordon Setter
Irish Setter
Irish Water Spaniel
Labrador Retriever
Pointer
Sussex Spaniel
Welsh Springer Spaniel
Vizsla
Weimaraner
Wirehaired Pointing
    Griffon

Hounds

Afghan Hound
American Foxhound
Basenji
Basset Hound

Beagle
Black and Tan Coonhound
Bloodhound
Borzoi
Dachshund
English Foxhound
Greyhound
Harrier
Ibizan Hound
Irish Wolfhound
Norwegian Elkhound
Otter Hound
Petite Basset Griffon
    Vendeen
Pharaoh Hound
Rhodesian Ridgeback
Saluki
Scottish Deerhound
Whippet

Working Dogs

Akita
Alaskan Malamute
Bernese Mountain Dog
Boxer
Bullmastiff
Doberman Pinscher
Giant Schnauzer
Great Dane
Great Pyrenees
Komondor
Kuvasz
Mastiff
Newfoundland
Portuguese Water Dog

Rottweiler
St. Bernard
Samoyed
Siberian Husky
Standard Schnauzer

Terriers

Airedale Terrier
American Staffordshire Terrier
Australian Terrier
Bedlington Terrier
Border Terrier
Bull Terrier
Cairn Terrier
Dandie Dinmont Terrier
Irish Terrier
Kerry Blue Terrier
Lakeland Terrier
Manchester Terrier
Miniature Schnauzer
Norfolk Terrier
Norwich Terrier
Scottish Terrier
Sealyham Terrier
Skye Terrier
Smooth Fox Terrier
Soft-Coated Wheaten Terrier
Staffordshire Bull Terrier
Welsh Terrier
West Highland White Terrier
Wire Fox Terrier

Toys

Affenpinscher
Brussels Griffon
Chihuahua
Chinese Crested
English Toy Spaniel
Italian Greyhound
Japanese Chin
Maltese

Miniature Pinscher
Papillon
Pekingese
Pomeranian
Pug
Shih Tzu
Silky Terrier
Toy Manchester Terrier
Toy Poodle
Yorkshire Terrier

Non-Sporting Dogs

Bichon Frise
Boston Terrier
Bulldog
Chinese Shar Pei
Chow Chow
Dalmatian
Finnish Spitz
French Bulldog
Keeshond
Lhasa Apso
Miniature Poodle
Standard Poodle
Schipperke
Tibetan Spaniel
Tibetan Terrier

Herding Dogs

Australian Cattle Dog
Australian Shepherd
Bearded Collie
Belgian Malinois
Belgian Sheepdog
Belgian Tervuren
Bouvier des Flandres
Briard
Cardigan Welsh Corgi
Collie
German Shepherd Dog
Old English Sheepdog
Pembroke Welsh Corgi
Puli
Shetland Sheepdog

Australian Kelpie
Border Collie
Canaan Dog
**Cavalier King Charles
Spaniel**

Greater Swiss Mountain
Dog
Miniature Bull Terrier
Shiba Inu
Spinoni Italiani

Same Dog, Different Size

Some breeds of dog appear in more than one size. Here are the most common breeds that vary in size. (Those names appearing in darker type show which breed is pictured in this guide.) Many other dogs may strongly resemble another breed except for size. For example, if you see a dog that's too small to be a Doberman Pinscher, you probably have met a Miniature Pinscher. Likewise, a dog too small to be an Airedale might be a Welsh Terrier. When in doubt, of course, ask the dog's owner.

Miniature Dachshund
Dachshund

Toy Manchester Terrier
Manchester Terrier

Miniature Schnauzer
Standard Schnauzer
Giant Schnauzer

Toy Poodle
Miniature Poodle
Standard Poodle

Miniature Bull Terrier
Bull Terrier

Italian Greyhound
Greyhound

A compact dog, the "Yorkie" used to be a ratter but now lives the life of a pampered companion dog. The smallest adult dog on record was a Yorkie who weighed 4 ounces and stood 2½ inches tall.

The **Silky Terrier** is a cross between the Yorkie and the Australian Terrier; it's a friendly, wiggly, persistent dog with a shorter coat.

> A dynamic, playful, spunky dog that will respond affectionately to attention.

a topknot bow often keeps hair from irritating the eyes

short, prick ears

small, docked tail

long, shiny steel-blue coat with tan hairs on the face and chest

dog's name: date: sighted ☐

The tiniest of the tiny, the Chihuahua is the oldest breed on the American continent, going back to 9th-century Mexico.

The **Long Coat Chihuahua** has a feathered, silky coat; the more common **Smooth Coat Chihuahua** has a short, flat coat.

> Loyal to the point of jealousy, these dogs are protective and don't take to strangers; they prefer only other Chihuahuas as companions and aren't intimidated by larger dogs.

bred in all colors and particolors

perky, pricked ears; very round eyes

plume tail for the Long Coat; sickle tail for the Smooth Coat

attentive to its owner and eager to please; can be alert and affectionate, or nervous and barky

dog's name: date: sighted ☐

In ancient China, the Pekingese was a palace guard dog, bred to look and act like a lion— its "terrifying" appearance was thought to scare off evil spirits. "Pekes" are long-lived dogs who demand constant grooming and affection.

all colors but albino and liver

pushed-in face; black muzzle with flat nose

> Loyal, fearless, and stubborn, Pekes can be barking and protective; not the ideal dog for young kids.

long, straight outercoat with thick undercoat

ring tail

frilly mane, as well as feathering on legs, toes, drop ears, and tail

short legs give a swaying roll to its walk

dog's name:	date:	sighted ☐

These spaniels were often traded for goods around the Mediterranean. The long, silky coat, which has no undercoat and is never shed, is pure white and falls to the ground from either side of a part running from the nose to the tail.

hair is often pulled over the eyes with a bow

> A very smart, alert, and delightful dog who enjoys kids.

flowing plume tail is carried over the back

large dark brown eyes with black rims

dog's name:	date:	sighted ☐

All varieties of this, the smallest spaniel, are identical except for color: There is the original, the **King Charles** (also called the **Black and Tan**); the **Prince Charles,** a tricolor; the **Blenheim,** white with chestnut-red markings; and the **Ruby,** a solid red.

The larger **Cavalier King Charles Spaniel** (shown here), has a flatter skull and a longer muzzle.

Very affectionate, cuddly dogs who may be timid; give them a little time to warm up to you.

feathered, hanging ears that measure 20 inches from one ear's tip to the other's

feathered "flag" tail droops down

square muzzle with a turned-up nose that creates a distinct stop

dog's name: date: sighted ☐

Originally from Pomerania, a region of the Baltic, the "Pom" was bred down in size over the centuries from a hefty, spitz-type sled dog to a dog that typically weighs four pounds. Sturdy watchdogs and obedient companions, this dog looks like a ruff of fur suspended on short legs.

A friendly, clever dog that enjoys showing off; has a surprisingly deep bark it sounds constantly.

like a typical spitz dog, it has a heavily feathered ring tail

fox-like face with a fox's small pricked ears

long, flowing double coat of any solid color or parti-color, with or without shadings or white markings

small, cat-like feet

dog's name: date: sighted ☐

Shih Tzu (pronounced "sheed zoo") means "lion" in Chinese, a name that might come from the dog who could change itself into a lion and travel with one of the Tibetan gods. A cousin of the Lhasa Apso, this breed dates back 1,300 years, though China permitted very few dogs to be taken from their country until the 1930s.

the Chinese say this dog's swaying walk looks like a goldfish

feathered ring tail carried almost as high as the head

Like most dogs from the Orient, the Shih Tzu is reserved around strangers; protective of and playful with those it knows. Be polite to instill trust when you meet.

prominent beard, whiskers, and topknot of hair

very long, floor-length coat, wavy or straight and of any color

dog's name: date: sighted ☐

Bred to "go to ground" in search of rodents, the Dachshund (German for "badger dog") is actually a terrier rather than a hound. Dachshunds are bred in two sizes: the larger **Standard** and the smaller **Miniature.** Each can have one of three coat types: **Wirehaired, Shorthaired** and **Longhaired**.

solid or particolor coat in many colors and shadings

Good watchdogs and loud barkers, but very affectionate pets, the Dachshund is intelligent and trainable, even if a little cocky.

long, tapering head and muzzle; drop ears

short legs and sharply protruding chest

dog's name: date: sighted ☐

This unusually sleek terrier was developed in England 300 years ago to be a rabbit hunter and rat catcher. Today it's happy to be an alert and energetic family member.

The **Toy Manchester Terrier** (shown here) is a shorter, slighter variety, which looks identical to the **Standard** except its ears aren't cropped.

coat is short and glossy; jet-black everywhere with clearly defined mahogany-tan markings

One of the least aggressive terriers; naturally well behaved, so its affection should be easy to win.

button ears, unless cropped

cat-like hind feet, with clear "pencil markings" of black

two middle toes are longer than the others

| dog's name: | date: | sighted ☐ |

Another China miniature, the Pug may be a smooth-coated version of the Pekingese. These are clean, playful dogs with the personality of a child who's never grown up. Pugs snort and grunt as well as bark, which has earned them the nickname "mopse," from the Dutch word for "grumble."

blunt and wrinkled face with black mask and ears

Spunky, mischief-making, and happiest when in a family's company; some Pugs can be hostile toward strangers.

rose ears

ring tail lies over a hip in one, or ideally, two curls

walks with a slight swaying or rolling motion; usually sits with its hind legs out to one side

short coat is either silver, apricot-fawn, or black

| dog's name: | date: | sighted ☐ |

Bichon Frise/Non-Sporting

Developed from the Maltese, the Bichon Frise (which means "curly lap-dog" in French; pronounced "bee-Shone free-Say") was traded among Mediterranean merchants, carried by sailors aboard ships, trained for circus routines, and pampered by the nobility of France and Spain.

velvety coat of white with some shadings of apricot or cream; loosely curled and trimmed or groomed into a frizzy "powder puff"

Well-mannered, cheerful companion with a sense of independence; should be glad to meet you.

black lips, black eye rims, dark skin under its coat

square body: its height should match the distance from the withers to the base of the tail

feathered gay tail

dog's name:	date:	sighted ☐

Lhasa Apso/Non-Sporting

Until the 12th century this dog was seen only in Tibet, where it was used as a temple guard dog. Lhasas were eventually presented to the rest of the world as gifts of the highest honor by Tibet's rulers. Some say that Lhasas can sense an avalanche before it occurs.

its long coat swishes across the floor as it walks; bred in all colors, but most commonly in honey or golden shades

Wary of strangers and quite assertive, the Lhasa is very trainable, appreciative of praise, and loving of those it trusts.

feathered ring tail

long drop ears with dark tips; excellent hearing

dog's name:	date:	sighted ☐

Originally the Norwich and the **Norfolk Terrier** were the same dog—a sturdy, short, ratting dog from Scotland. Eventually they were separated into two breeds by virtue of their ears. The Norwich's prick ears stand up (like the "w" in its name); the Norfolk's drop ears are folded ("folded" sounds like Nor*folk*).

small almond eyes and a foxy muzzle give an "impish" look

Both have terrier charm, fearlessness, and spirit; a properly trained dog won't be aggressive or shy.

wiry, straight coats on either dog may be red, wheaten, black and tan, or grizzle

short, docked tail, held very high

ruff of hair at the neck

| dog's name: | date: | sighted ☐ |

The Cairn Terrier is a short-legged sporting dog, bred to go after rodents and foxes, who now makes a good living as a companion animal. Perhaps the most famous Cairn is Toto, Dorothy's dog in *The Wizard of Oz*.

The **Australian Terrier**'s body shape and weight are like the Cairn's but its coat is steel-blue and tan.

shaggy, weather-resistant double coat in any color but white

Both are friendly companions but true terriers—restless, inquisitive, even maddening at times; they should greet your invitation to play with enthusiasm.

eyebrows protect the eyes

large forefeet, on which the dog appears to lean its body

| dog's name: | date: | sighted ☐ |

In the early 1600s, a Spanish ship crashed on the rocks of Skye, a Scottish island. The several Maltese on board swam to shore and bred with local terriers, creating the Skye Terrier. Its extraordinary 5½-inch-long coat is parted down the middle from its nose to its tail.

very feathered ears, either drop or prick, but always black

Wary of strangers and often stubborn, this dog does not do well with other dogs; however, it can be a fine companion if raised properly.

long, hanging tail usually carried in a shallow arc

coat colors may be black, blue, cream, fawn, or gray

twice as long as it is tall

dog's name: date: sighted ☐

The "Westie" is an all-white terrier bred in Scotland to hunt small mammals. It's an alert, courageous dog that needs as much training as affection.

The **Sealyham Terrier** is another white member of the Terrier group, but the "Sealie" possesses a beard, longer muzzle, drop ears, and a wavier coat with tan, lemon, or badger markings on the head.

face thickly covered with hair

Affectionate, playful, mischievous dogs that like to make friends; be sure to be introduced.

short tail carried high in a proud manner

though its coat is white, there's black on the lips, eye rims, nails, foot pads, and skin

dog's name: date: sighted ☐

The "Scottie" is only about 100 years old, and is a close relative of the West Highland White, Cairn, and Dandie Dinmont terriers. Scotties are charming and even "conceited" companions, whose intensely protective and scrappy nature requires firm training.

most popular coat is black, but also bred in sandy, wheaten, gray, and brindle

bushy eyebrows above almond-shaped eyes

Fearless, headstrong dogs that rarely back down; they tend to fight other dogs and often threaten strangers. Be cautious and avoid potential problems.

short, jaunty gay tail points upward

front feet larger than hind feet

hair on the face is combed forward in a long beard and moustache

dog's name:	date:	sighted ☐

These intelligent, "condo-size big dogs" were bred as cattle-herders over 900 years ago. There are two types of Corgis: the **Cardigan Welsh Corgi** (shown here) is a slightly taller, longer dog with a long, white-tipped brush tail; the **Pembroke Welsh Corgi** has a naturally short or docked tail.

herding instinct is so strong, they'll often try to herd children, ducks, or bicyclers

rounded bat ears

Tireless, talented, and totally devoted to their family; they are sometimes wary of strangers and protective of property.

coat colors can be red, sable, black and tan; Pembrokes are often fawn; Cardigans can also be brindle or blue merle

dog's name:	date:	sighted ☐

These terriers, not yet members of the AKC, were developed 200 years ago by Reverend Jack Russell, who wanted a fox-size dog to pursue foxes underground. These dogs come in two coat types: the **Smooth-Coat** (short, flat hair) and the **Rough-Coat** (longer, bristly hair).

impressive ability to jump straight up in the air

Affectionate with people, tireless, and persistent; they often need obedience training.

V-shaped drop ears

very energetic and excited; would rather dig than rest in your lap

coat is mostly white with black or tan markings

dog's name: date: sighted ☐

The only terrier not originally from the British Isles, the Schnauzer is now recognized as three breeds. The **Standard Schnauzer** is the medium-size ancestor, a fine ratter from Germany. The **Giant Schnauzer** was developed with Great Dane stock to herd cattle. The **Miniature Schnauzer** was bred down in size to be a smaller guard and companion.

telltale bristly moustache and beard (*Schnauze* means "muzzle" in German)

large eyebrows

The Miniature tolerates other dogs and is least aggressive. The Standard needs a firm, attentive owner or it may threaten others. The Giant is happiest as the only dog around since it will challenge other dogs.

coarse, wiry coat can be black, black and silver, or salt and pepper with tan shading

dog's name: date: sighted ☐

Tthese alert dogs were originally bred for fox hunting, but now they make terrific if somewhat edgy companions, ready to pursue the slightest noise or motion. The **Smooth Fox Terrier** has flat, thick hair; the **Wire Fox Terrier** has a kinkier outercoat with a soft undercoat, as well as a beard around its muzzle.

tail is usually docked, held straight and high

Although these dogs do enjoy people, they are very aggressive toward, and often fight with, other dogs.

round, dark eyes should be "full of fire"

"steel spring legs" enable these sturdy dogs to bounce up and down for a long time

coat is mostly white with tan, black, or brown markings; there's often a saddle

dog's name: _____ date: _____ sighted ☐

Named for the woodcock, a small gamebird they were trained to hunt, the first "cockers" are said to have arrived in America aboard the *Mayflower*. Once the same dog, they're now two separate breeds: the smaller, swifter **American Cocker Spaniel** and the original **English Cocker Spaniel.**

beautiful coat is black, parti-color, or any other solid; when groomed long, it swishes like a skirt around its moving legs

Loving, alert, and courageous; because of overbreeding, some dogs have behavior problems such as biting and submissive urination; ask for owner's help when meeting.

very long ears

deep stop on a square muzzle

docked tail that's usually wagging eagerly

dog's name: _____ date: _____ sighted ☐

Members of the spaniel family of dogs, Poodles are bred in three sizes: the **Toy Poodle** is under 10 inches tall, the **Miniature Poodle** is between 10 and 15 inches tall, and the **Standard Poodle,** the original variety, stands over 15 inches tall. The name comes from the German word *Pudel,* meaning "one who splashes in the water."

very clean dogs, who do like mud puddles

Extremely bright and eager learners, Poodles love children and, even more, the chance to show off; some Toys are nervous and some Standards are protective, so use your own good dog sense.

non-shedding, curly coat in most colors, commonly black, white, gray, brown, and apricot

pompon tail is part of fancy haircut

dog's name: date: sighted ☐

These long-lived sheepherding dogs come from the Shetland Islands of Scotland and look like miniature Collies. "Shelties" are loyal, intelligent, sensitive, sometimes barky, and very eager to learn; they love training and excel at obedience.

semi-prick ears when alert; drop ears when resting

Affectionate with family members, but can be distant around strangers; win over a Sheltie with a game of catch.

luxurious double-coat comes in black, blue merle, sable, black and white, black and tan, or tricolor with white markings

cleans its legs and feet like a cat

smooth face, feet, and stifles, but otherwise thickly feathered with prominent apron, trousers, and brush tail

dog's name: date: sighted ☐

Now the national dog of England, this hefty, short-coated dog was originally bred for fighting. A compressed muzzle gives the Bulldog a tendency to snore, wheeze, and suffer during hot weather.

The **French Bulldog** is a much slighter, smaller, bat-eared version.

coat colors include brindles, reds, and beige

large head, heavily wrinkled head and face, small rose ears

Loving, affectionate, and courageous; if food is around, a Bulldog might not be a good sharer.

stocky chest with two loose folds of the dewlap at the neck

the lower jaw curves up and extends beyond the upper jaw

the shorter hind legs and broad body give it a shuffling, swaying walk

dog's name: date: sighted ☐

The smallest of the hunting hounds, Beagles are divided into two types, according to size: the **Thirteen-Inch** (under 13 inches tall) and the **Fifteen-Inch** (between 13 and 15 inches tall). At one time, the Pocket Beagle was small enough to fit in a hunter's coat pocket. Snoopy may be the world's most famous Beagle.

has a melodious voice, which it likes to use, especially when alone

tall, tapering gay tail

Tireless, agreeable, pack-oriented animals, Beagles enjoy the company of other dogs and children; good training brings out the best in them.

its body is as long as it is tall

short coat of the typical hound combination: white, black, and tan

straight front legs with round, cat-like feet

dog's name: date: sighted ☐

The Bedlington's lamb-like look disguises its background as a hunter of vermin, fox, and otter. Its Whippet ancestors give the dog a light walk, a tucked-up belly, and an arching back.

deeply wrinkled brows and soulful eyes (with the pink lower eyelids showing) create a "sad" look that masks the dog's real intelligence

Though loyal and charming, they may be stubborn and bullying; use good sense when bringing dogs together.

hanging ears with white fringe

topknot of hair is a lighter color

curly coat is usually clipped; colors are liver, blue, or sand, or a bi-color of any of those with tan

curved, tapering tail

dog's name: date: sighted ☐

The Basset Hound is said to be "half a dog tall and twice a dog long." A great sniffer, its nose can rival a Bloodhound's; for its size, its ears are the longest of any breed. Often used in tracking game through fields, Bassets are slow moving but very persistent, with a deep distinctive bark.

droopy appearance: big dewlaps; upper lip hangs over lower lips; prominent flews

Very well behaved and good natured, this dog enjoys kids in particular; take a Basset for a long romp in the country.

long, tapered tail carried high when moving

hound-colored coat with wrinkled skin on short, sturdy legs

dog's name: date: sighted ☐

Boston Terrier/Non-Sporting — MED

One of only a dozen dogs created in the U.S., the Boston Terrier was developed just over 100 years ago by crossing the English Terrier and the Bulldog. The lively Boston Terrier is said to have the personality of a "small aristocrat."

colors are brindle and white or black and white

bat ears, often cropped

short tail is either screw or straight

the eyes face directly forward, separated by a white muzzle and blaze

full jowls

dog's name: date: sighted ☐

Basenji/Hound — MED

Originally called the Congo Barkless Dog, the Basenji comes from Africa, where his name is the Swahili word for "savage." A most unusual and ancient dog, the Basenji has a deer's grace and beauty, a cat's curiosity and grooming habits, a racehorse's trotting gait—and a yodel instead of a bark.

ring tail

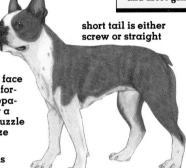

wrinkled forehead above a proud or often surprised expression; often cocks its head to the side when something's caught its attention

colors include chestnut, black, or black and tan, but all have white feet, chest, and tip of the tail

dog's name: date: sighted ☐

33

American Staffordshire Terrier

The "Amstaff," whose ancestry is half Bulldog, is one of the largest terriers. Often incorrectly called a Pit Bull, this powerful dog has many positive characteristics. With good training, these dogs are docile, energetic, and can be good companions for kids.

The **Staffordshire Bull Terrier** is a slighter, smaller version of this breed.

rounded, broad head with a medium-size muzzle

prick ears (sometimes cropped) or half-rose

Firm training brings out its best nature, but it can act viciously if provoked and may be unfriendly toward other dogs and cats; make sure the dog's owner is present at your meeting.

coat can be any color but black and tan, liver, or mostly white

dog's name: date: sighted ☐

Keeshond/Non-Sporting

Another spitz-type dog, the Keeshond (pronounced "kaze-hawnd") was once used on canal boats by the Dutch. The English jokingly called this dog an "Overweight Pomeranian." Bred as a companion dog for the last century, the Keeshond is an ideal family member and sensible watchdog.

a "fur coat" of long hairs, silver with black tips

Very alert, gentle, devoted, and eager, these can be one-person dogs; see if you can coax it into playing.

eyes have black spectacles

smirky grin, like other spitz dogs

ring tail, curled tightly over the back

thick trousers

dog's name: date: sighted ☐

Bearded Collie/Herding MED

Similar in appearance to the Old English Sheepdog, the "Beardie" is a smaller, slighter dog with a tail that isn't bobbed. Also called Mountain or Highland Collies, Beardies worked as drovers, moving herds of cattle.

A joyous, unspoiled breed, known for its wonderful disposition; the friendly, bright expression speaks for itself.

fringe tail, carried high when excited

feet usually lift just high enough to clear the ground when walking, so they appear to be gliding

shaggy double coat; colors are black, blue, fawn or brown, with white markings possible

dog's name: date: sighted ☐

Brittany/Sporting MED

Once called the Brittany Spaniel, this is a vigorous, smaller version of a setter developed for hunting in France. It is a true spaniel with a fine sense of smell, but it also possesses a setter's ability to point and retrieve.

heavy eyebrows (to protect the eyes from stickers when running) above amber eyes

Persistent though trainable, the Brittany has a very keen desire to please; since this dog needs work to channel its energy, offer some outdoor adventure.

nose can be fawn, tan, light brown, or pink (but not black)

naturally short tail, or docked to four inches

coat is either liver and white or orange and white; usually has lots of ticking

dog's name: date: sighted ☐

Until 1892, when they were divided into two separate breeds, Cockers and Springers were born in the same litter of puppies—size was all that separated them. "Springers" are the larger of the two breeds.

The **Welsh Springer Spaniel** is a smaller dog, red and white in color, with shorter ears.

A happy, frisky, ball-playing dog who is quick to learn; both lovable and loving, a Springer should be eager to meet you and your dog.

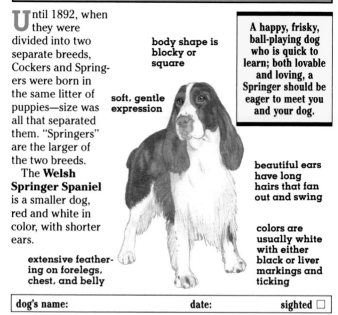

body shape is blocky or square

soft, gentle expression

beautiful ears have long hairs that fan out and swing

colors are usually white with either black or liver markings and ticking

extensive feathering on forelegs, chest, and belly

dog's name: _____   date: _____   sighted ☐

The Border Collie was the reindeer-herding dog of the Vikings. Developed in Scotland, Borders possess a keen ability to control herds of sheep. By "showing eye," they can move or stop sheep with a stare. Superb obedience dogs, they have a keen drive to perform well; without the chance, they can become bored and difficult.

Very energetic dogs some call "workaholics"; they're great with kids, so help a Border Collie burn up energy with games. Don't be surprised if one tries to round up you and your friends!

coat is white with black, blue, red, chocolate, or merle; a variety of looks can be found

dense coat with feathering on chest, belly, and legs

thick brush tail

dog's name: _____   date: _____   sighted ☐

The national dog of Norway, these spitz-type dogs of wolf ancestry have a long history of alliances with people—they accompanied the Vikings on their travels. A rugged, able dog, the Elkhound has been used to hunt bear, lynx, elk, and other wild game; to pull sleds; and to herd and protect flocks.

broad head with prick ears, and a serious face

A happy, gentle family member, with an independent spirit that can be difficult.

very vocal dog; its yelps, yaps, and yips are very expressive and an attentive human should be able to interpret them

furry ring tail curls tightly over the back

double coat of gray with a black muzzle, ears, and tail tip; lighter undercoat

dog's name:	date:	sighted ☐

Once called the "gladiator of the dog world" and pitted against bulls and other dogs, the "BT" is now an even-tempered companion. It is bred in two sizes, the **Standard** and the **Miniature;** both sizes come in two color varieties, **white** and **colored.** These dogs are athletic and rowdy. They need firm training.

triangle-shaped eyes set close together on an egg-shaped face

Friendly, a well-trained BT will be great with kids; like any terrier, might take some time getting to know you and might spar with another dog.

tapering tail, carried horizontally

Roman head and nose (no stop, just a flat slope from the top of the head to the tip of the nose)

broad, muscular chest

short, flat coat with tight skin

dog's name:	date:	sighted ☐

Whippet/Hound — MED

Bred a century ago to chase rabbits, the Whippet looks like a small Greyhound. A powerful runner who can reach 35 miles an hour within a few seconds, it doubles up its body so that the hind legs pass in front of the front feet. Graceful, but not as fragile as it looks, the Whippet doesn't shed and hardly barks.

> Good with kids and seldom mean, the Whippet is a naturally quiet companion, happy just to snuggle; owners say their dogs love blankets, and sometimes "unmake" the bed just to curl up.

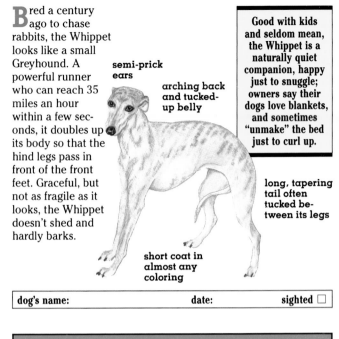

semi-prick ears

arching back and tucked-up belly

long, tapering tail often tucked between its legs

short coat in almost any coloring

dog's name: date: sighted ☐

Samoyed/Working — MED

These are the dogs that helped to discover the South Pole in 1911. The "Sammy," known as the "little white teddy bear" of the dog world, is perhaps the closest relative to the earliest dogs on earth. It was used by nomadic tribes for herding, guarding, pulling, and just plain companionship.

> Friendly, gentle, adaptable, very smart, and very loyal to a loving family.

nose color can lighten in winter

long brush tail carried over the back

black lips slightly curve at the corners to create the "Samoyed smile"

pure white, cream, or biscuit colored; should have a silver sheen

feathered, hare-like foot

dog's name: date: sighted ☐

Chow Chow/Non-Sporting　　MED

With the mane of a lion and a scowling bear's face, the compact-bodied Chow was developed 2,000 years ago in China to guard temples, fighting off both evil spirits and human intruders. Now the dog is bred purely as a family companion, a job it takes very seriously.

only dog with blue-black tongue (the flews and the roof of the mouth are also black)

brush tail arches over the back

Although well-behaved, Chows have very independent, willful personalities; many can be openly aggressive toward other people or dogs. Do not meet a Chow without its owner.

coat can be any one color, usually black, red, tawny, or blue

| dog's name: | date: | sighted ☐ |

Labrador Retriever/Sporting　　MED

One of the most popular dogs in America, the "Lab" comes from Newfoundland. A talented and versatile dog, Labs are also used in rescue and search teams, on drug-sniffing patrols, and as guide dogs.

short, flat coat is either black, yellow, or chocolate

Active, outgoing, with a great deal of personality and affection; a dog with high energy and high exercise needs. A wonderful dog for kids.

broad head with medium-size hanging ears

otter tail, round and thickly furred

The **Chesapeake Bay Retriever,** a similarly shaped water dog, has webbed feet and a kinky, waterproof coat of dark brown or tan.

| dog's name: | date: | sighted ☐ |

Developed by an Inuit people of Siberia for pulling sleds and herding reindeer, "Siberians" (don't call them "Huskies," which just means any sort of Arctic sled dog) went with Admiral Byrd on his expeditions to the Antarctic. Their great endurance has made Siberians the principal members of dog-sled teams.

head often has a variety of masks, blazes, and other markings

An independent, gentle friend to own or visit, but a dog whose tendency to roam must be checked.

dark-ringed, almond-shaped eyes can be brown, blue, or one of each

howls rather than barks

weatherproof double coat (which sheds a lot), in most colors from black to pure white

brush tail, held over the back when excited, otherwise hangs down

dog's name: date: sighted ☐

The Airedale, from England, is one of the largest terriers. A fine swimmer and an able hunting companion, it has been used to find and corner otters, stags, and even bears. This versatile, faithful, protective animal has also served as a guard and police dog in Europe.

V-shaped drop ears

Can be stubborn and aloof, so this dog needs firm and kind training from puppyhood.

bushy beard is combed forward

stout tail is usually docked and held up so the tip is as high as the top of the dog's head

dense, wiry coat is black with tan on the head, legs, and underbody

dog's name: date: sighted ☐

Dalmatian/Non-Sporting — MED

The Dalmatian may be named after Dalmatia, a European region on the Adriatic coast where these dogs were known to travel with Gypsies; but its ancient origins are unclear. The "Dal" has been nicknamed Plum Pudding Dog and Fire House Dog. It has an excellent memory, loves horses, and excels at many kinds of work.

eyes are dark if the coat has black spots; amber or even blue if liver spots

Very active, gentle dogs that are quiet but dependable watchdogs; they can sense a would-be friend, so show your good intentions.

Dals are born white; the spots begin to show up a few weeks later

round, small feet with arched toes looks like a cat's

white coat with spots of either black or liver

dog's name: date: sighted ☐

Collie/Herding — MED

Originally these dogs, from Scotland and northern England, were primarily coal colored and were known as "Coally Dogs." The more popular **Rough Collie** has an abundant outer-coat. The **Smooth Collie** looks smaller because of its smooth, flat coat. Lassie is probably the world's most famous Collie.

wedge-shaped head: long, tapering skull with a blunt muzzle

Loves children, but does demand an extra measure of attention and exercise; may be shy at first around strangers, so be patient and allow the dog to greet you.

very expressive, small, semi-prick ears

very small, almond-shaped eyes

brush tail

coat colors are sable and white, tricolor, blue merle, or white

dog's name: date: sighted ☐

41

Golden Retriever/Sporting — MED

Created for hunting waterfowl, the "golden" is a great swimmer but has become a favorite dog around the world for its faithful, antic, affectionate companionship. A dog of high energy and high intelligence, the golden excels at obedience and is often employed as a guide dog, scent tracker, and ideal visitor for the ill or elderly.

handsome coat of gold color, from nearly white to almost red

Very friendly, extremely pettable, and attention craving; takes to nearly every game, particularly ones that involve carrying something in the mouth.

dogs possess the "golden paw," a way of using their front paws to grab or reach

fringe tail, apron, trousers, feathered legs

dog's name: date: sighted ☐

Boxer/Working — MED

The Boxer's name comes from its "boxing" style of fighting, which it used in hunting and in fighting bulls. Its square head with an upturned nose and lower jaw that curves above the upper jaw gives the Boxer a one-of-a-kind look.

ears are either drop or cropped to a tall point

Patient with children and wary of strangers, the Boxer is fearless and strong; win its friendship first, then prepare for energetic play.

with its very short, docked tail, the Boxer wags its whole body when excited

broad barrel chest

very short coat is fawn or brindle with white markings

dog's name: date: sighted ☐

Old English Sheepdog/Herding   MED

The "Bobtail" dog of the English countryside was used to drive cattle herds to market. Since owners didn't have to pay tax on working dogs, they bobbed the tails of these Sheepdogs to prove their working status. This is an unmistakable breed, with a thick, shaggy coat that protects it against heat, cold, and dampness.

these dogs have a bear-like shuffle — both legs on the same side move forward at once

A playful, bouncy, boisterous dog that's excellent with kids; protects them like a flock.

eyes are often concealed by hair

a very loud and unusual bark

dog's name: date: sighted ☐

Weimaraner/Sporting   MED

Bred in Weimar, Germany, the "Weimie" is a sporting dog, a remarkably active, inventive animal that needs lots of exercise and guidance to bring out its exceptional gifts for companionship.

The **Vizsla** (pronounced "Veezh-loh"), or Hungarian Pointer, is a similar looking but much smaller dog with a solid golden-rust color.

eyes are light amber, gray, or blue-gray

A very friendly, gentle dog with great intelligence and a mind of its own; should be glad for your company.

short, bobbed tail is in constant motion

very short gray coat

dog's name: date: sighted ☐

43

Foxhound/Hound

The first Foxhounds were brought to America in 1650. George Washington imported these dogs as well. Here, the **English Foxhound** was crossbred to produce the **American Foxhound** (shown here), a lighter and faster dog. Both were bred for foxhunting: Hunters on horseback followed packs of these dogs into the fields.

short coat in the usual hound colors: white, black, and tan

A robust pack animal that likes its own kind, this dog is cheerful, slightly hard to train, and happiest outdoors.

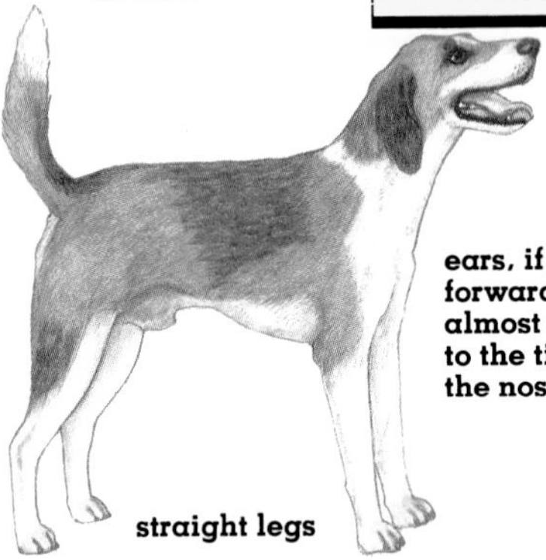

ears, if held forward, can almost reach to the tip of the nose

straight legs

dog's name: date: sighted ☐

German Shepherd Dog/Herding

The Shepherd is one of the most popular and useful breeds in the world, working as a police, herding, guard, scenting, and guide dog. Also known as Alsatians, these dogs are only about a hundred years old, bred from German Sheepdogs and native wolves.

thick brush tail carried low, almost to the ground

A properly trained Shepherd should never be aggressive, but it may be shy; use good judgment. These are typically lively, courageous companions.

thick, double coat, usually black with brown, though can be tan, gray, sable, or black; usually has a darker saddle

very expressive, intelligent face with large, prick ears, called tulip ears

dog's name: date: sighted ☐

The Irish Setter is a lean, chestnut-red dog with ample feathering all along its body. It is one of three setters: The **Gordon Setter,** from Scotland, is a calmer black-and-tan version of this dog. The especially trainable **English Setter** is usually white flecked with lemon, black, orange, liver, or chestnut.

narrow head with medium-size stop and point at the top of the skull

hanging ears

Outgoing, devoted, sometimes a little reckless, a setter needs lots of space, exercise, and competent training; may act aloof with some strangers—make friends by playing a game of catch.

tapering fringe tail, carried level with the back

dog's name: date: sighted ☐

Pointers "stand game:" At the first sight of the quarry the dog stops, raises a leg, holds its tail erect, and holds its position—aimed at the quarry—while the hunter runs ahead to shoot.

The other two pointers are the **German Short-Haired Pointer** and the **German Wire-Haired Pointer.** Both are liver in color with white markings and a docked tail.

fine, short coat, mostly white with liver markings (or lemon, orange, or black)

hare-footed with a light and sneaky step

Dignified field dogs, these animals are affectionate with family members, though shy around strangers and jealous of other dogs; they're simply happiest when working and exercising.

very clear stop

tapering tail held level with body

dog's name: date: sighted ☐

The "African Lion Hound," originally from South Africa, was used in packs to hunt lions. Both a gaze- and a scent-hound, it uses its eyes if it can see the game, and its nose if it can't. This is the only dog with "a snake on its back"—a "ridge" of hair, growing in the opposite direction, follows the dog's backbone from the shoulder to the hip.

two "crowns," or whorls, at the top of the ridge

forehead wrinkles when the dog perks to attention

Although they do like kids and are good family dogs, they are reserved and watchful, barking only when they have a good reason.

tail, as with most hounds, hangs down between its legs

sleek coat ranges from light- to red-wheaten in color

dog's name: _____ date: _____ sighted ☐

The Black and Tan is one of several dogs trained to hunt possums and raccoons; others, differing mostly in size and coloring, include the **Bluetick, English, Redbone,** and **Treeing Walker Coonhounds.** These scent-hounds are determined rather than fast. When they've finally treed an animal, they "bark up," signaling the hunter with their voices.

pumpkinseed marking over each rather droopy eye

Quiet dogs (except when on the hunt), gentle and friendly, although not always interested in playing—respect that.

long, soft hanging ears that extend well beyond the nose

prominent flews and dewlaps

black "pencil marks" on the toes

dog's name: _____ date: _____ sighted ☐

Doberman Pinscher/Working — LGE

Louis Dobermann created this sleek, powerful dog by cross-breeding Rottweilers, Great Danes, German Shepherds, and maybe a few other breeds. The "Dobies'" intelligence has made them popular as police- and watch-dogs.

The **Miniature Pinscher,** or "Min-pin," with its high-stepping gait, looks like a very small Dobie.

Courageous and aggressive when necessary, the Dobie can still be an attentive family dog if brought up lovingly and given plenty to do; never meet one without the owner present.

straight back ends in a docked tail

blunt muzzle

coat is black and rust, fawn, red, or blue

cat-like feet

dog's name: date: sighted ☐

Bernese Mountain Dog/Working — LGE

There are four breeds of Swiss Mountain Dogs, the most popular in America being this one with the long, silky coat. An extremely good-natured, easy-going, handsome dog, the Bernese has worked as a drover, watchdog, and draft dog during its 2,000 years of existence.

One of the most cheerful, smart, faithful, and lovable companions; needs lots of attention to be happy.

white is always on the tail tip, face, and chest

loves cold weather

dramatic tricolor coat: jet black with russet (light brown) and white markings

bushy tail

dog's name: date: sighted ☐

Powerful, compact dogs, "Rotties" were first used to protect traveling German butchers and their cattle herds. Although they are used as police dogs and many have been provoked into becoming aggressive animals, a well-trained Rottweiler should be very sweet-natured, and eager for a kid's company.

massive head

pumpkinseed over each eye

A natural guard dog that can be very aggressive toward other dogs; take your time when befriending a Rottweiler and avoid any that seem hostile or that growl.

hind feet are longer than the forefeet

short black coat with tan on the cheeks, muzzle, chest, and feet

"pencil marks" on the toes

dog's name: date: sighted ☐

Japan has declared the Akita one of its National Treasures; when a child is born, people send small statues of an Akita to symbolize happiness. These are spitz-type dogs of exceptional poise and beauty, although they have been used to hunt deer and boar and to fight other dogs. Helen Keller brought the first Akita to America.

tall prick ears set wide apart

thick tail carried over the back

Protective of family members and often aggressive toward other dogs, these strong, loyal companions can be either calm or spirited; read the dog's body language and take your cue.

coarse outer coat in any color; often with markings and clearly defined mask

dog's name: date: sighted ☐

Bloodhound/Hound LGE

Since the third century, Bloodhounds have been considered the best sniffers in the canine world—they have been known to track a human's trail for over a hundred miles. This long-eared, droopy-eyed, solemn-faced dog is unmistakable, and its singing ability is legendary.

top of the skull is very tall

prominent flews and dewlap

One of the most docile dogs; affectionate, shy, sensitive, quick to learn but often stubborn, the Bloodhound is never quarrelsome with people or other dogs.

usually wags its tail

loose skin; coat can be black and tan, red and tan, red, or tawny

its long ears cup the scent to its nose as the dog tracks

dog's name: date: sighted ☐

St. Bernard/Working LGE

These bear-like dogs worked with monks as four-dog rescue teams in the mountains between Switzerland and Italy. Many are reported to be able to predict avalanches.

The **Shorthaired** variety of this breed seems smaller because of its flatter coat.

drooping lower eyelids

One of the most soft-hearted dogs; always happy and responsive to children; needs extra room to frolic.

roof of the mouth is black

massive, broad head with a large stop

thick bushy tail

coat can be white with red, red with white, or brindle with white

dog's name: date: sighted ☐

The "Newf" from Newfoundland, Canada, may be a cross between a Great Pyrenees and a Black English Retriever. One of the most massive dogs, it is also one of the most easygoing family dogs. Since Victorian times, Newfs have been portrayed as the child's protector and companion. Nana, in "Peter Pan," is a Newf—a perfect nanny dog.

a muscular, strong body, often weighing 150 pounds

Agreeable, eager, playful, kind dogs who love company, other pets, and the chance to do what they do best— swim and play; don't exert these dogs in hot weather.

waterproof, heavy coat of black or brown; a black-and-white version is called a Landseer

webbed, cat-like feet

dog's name: date: sighted ☐

These are the sled dogs of Alaska, named after the Mahlemuts, an Inuit tribe. "Mals" are also employed to hunt polar bear and wolf, and to guard and herd caribou. Their undercoat protects them from the cold. A spitz-type dog, they are commonly mistaken for the much smaller Siberian Husky.

eyes are always brown (unlike Siberians)

Independent thinkers, and happiest outdoors, Mals are very affectionate with people; they are inclined to be aggressive with other dogs.

brush tail curled over its back

dense, woolly coat ranges from gray to black with a white underbelly

wolf-like face with a clear mask

Mals rarely bark; they "woo-woo" instead

dog's name: date: sighted ☐

Another hound from ancient Egypt, the Afghan was used for hunting large animals such as snow leopards. These elegant-looking dogs are both spirited and sensitive; they need a little extra care, not only in grooming but also in training.

The **Saluki,** one of the oldest known breeds, is slighter, with a short coat except for the tail and ears.

very swift, beautiful galloping gait

Nice with other dogs, but not likely to be outgoing with strangers.

hair down the back is short and smooth

tail is sparsely feathered and ringed at the tip

long, silky coat in any color, with plenty of feathering except on the face and spine

dog's name: date: sighted ☐

The Greyhound first appeared 5,000 years ago as a dog of Egyptian royalty. It has been clocked at speeds of 44 miles per hour. Greyhounds rescued from their short careers in dog racing can make wonderful pets, although they need a good run each day.

The **Italian Greyhound** is a miniature version of this dog.

folded ears that, when alert, cock to the sides

Often shy and reserved; let the dog warm up to you, then offer to go for a run.

from its pointed nose to its whip tail, the entire body is long and sleek

may have markings, a multi-colored coat, or a solid coat of black, white, red, or blue

very straight front legs

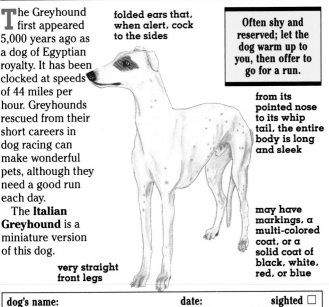

dog's name: date: sighted ☐

Borzoi/Hound

The Borzoi (the word means "swift" in Russian) is also called the Russian Wolfhound. A sleek, speedy, aristocratic gaze-hound, it was once used for wolf hunting but now makes a calm enough companion for the family willing to give extensive obedience training, grooming, and running.

ears folded back, almost touching each other behind the head

long and elegant Roman nose

Although unlikely to be hostile, the Borzoi is often affectionate only with family members.

curving back and a bony frame

coat is long and silky, often wavy; in any color — usually white with markings

very long, feathered tail, carried low

dog's name:	date:	sighted ☐

Great Pyrenees/Working

The "Great Dog of the Mountain," the "Pyr" is a giant dog that needs surprisingly little exercise and space for its size. Traditionally these animals worked as sled dogs in winter and cart dogs in summer, or as guardians for flocks of sheep. Jokingly nicknamed a "mat dog," the Pyr loves to be outside, lying on the doormat.

long, heavy, protective white coat, either straight or wavy

A very affectionate, gentle, devoted dog; rarely fights with other dogs.

dark "badger" markings around the eyes

double set of dewclaws on the hind legs

rolling, ambling gait

dog's name:	date:	sighted ☐

The "Apollo of Dogs," the Great Dane is an ancient, Mastiff-like breed popularized in Germany (not Denmark). It has worked as a boar hunter and a body-guard, but now it is bred for companion-ship, at which it excels. These short-lived dogs continue to grow for almost two years; only the Irish Wolfhound stands taller.

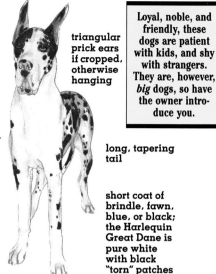

triangular prick ears if cropped, otherwise hanging

Loyal, noble, and friendly, these dogs are patient with kids, and shy with strangers. They are, however, *big* dogs, so have the owner intro-duce you.

long, tapering tail

short coat of brindle, fawn, blue, or black; the Harlequin Great Dane is pure white with black "torn" patches

dog's name: date: sighted ☐

Dogs of this breed stand over 32 inches tall, but are slighter than the other giant dogs. Bred 2,000 years ago as a protector of herds and a hunter of elk, the Irish Wolfhound needs daily exer-cise, loves to chase and gallop, and likes to lie together with other Wolf-hounds in heaps. It is the national dog of Ireland.

coat colors are gray, brindle, red, black, fawn, or pure white

little rose ears

A docile, trust-worthy, kid-oriented dog; never aggressive, and not even very suspicious of strangers.

hair is espe-cially wiry around the dark-rimmed eyes, and under the jaw

extremely long sickle tail

dog's name: date: sighted ☐

The Most Common Mutts

Although any two dogs that aren't too different in size can produce puppies, certain mutt types do appear quite often. Some purebred dogs are very common and more likely to escape and mate with neighbor dogs, while other breeds are more scarce and less available for random mating.

Here are some of the most common neighborhood mutts. On the blank pages of the FIELD GUIDE you might draw or attach photographs of the mutts you meet. Remember, what follows isn't official—it's just a way to group and identify some of the mutts you're likely to see.

The Black-and-Tan

Humane Society experts say that sixty percent of the dogs brought to shelters are "shepherd mixes," meaning one of the dog's parents was probably a purebred or mixed-breed German Shepherd. The basic black-and-tan is almost a universal dog— what randomly bred dogs will create after many litters. This mutt has short hair (an easy coat to maintain), a medium build, and a long tail.

The Retriever-of-Sorts

This mutt usually has a Labrador Retriever some-
where in its family tree. Most often it has a
medium-to-long black coat, a stocky chest, and
probably a splotch of white on the chest or feet.

Close relatives of these mutts are those with a
Golden Retriever in their background. A "golden's"
genes will give these mutts longer coats, feathering
on the legs and   chest, and possibly a fawn
or red-brown
color.

The Terrier Two-fer

These mutts are usually small or medium size
with a scraggly, scruffy, any-colored coat and
some feathering on the legs and chest. Often one
parent is purebred terrier; but in most cases, the
dog's ancestry is pretty mixed up.

The Mini-Mix

It's hard to group all the Poodle, Beagle, and Miniature Schnauzer mixes together, but there is a group of smallish mutts that don't seem very terrier-like and that come in all colors and coat lengths.

Two crossbreeds that people throughout the country are encouraging are the cock-a-poo (a Cocker Spaniel/Miniature Poodle mix) and the peke-a-poo (a Pekingese/Miniature Poodle mix). Who knows, they might achieve official breed status in the future.

The Collie-Combo

This is the mutt with the long nose and the beautifully wavy coat with patches of sable, black, white, or brown. The narrow Collie nose, with its blunt point, is usually lost in the mixture.

Here are fill-in pages so you can include individual dogs you meet. The dogs may be additions to your life list of breeds that are not shown in the FIELD GUIDE. Or they may be your friends' and neighbors' dogs, in which case your extra information might be useful for dog-sitting jobs. Take a snapshot or make a colored pencil sketch of the dog. Complete the page as much as you can, adding your own remarks about the dog's temperament and key features.

Breed: **Group:**

Photo or sketch:

Name: ———————————————————
Size:————————————————————
Coat length and color: ——————————————

———————————————————————

Special markings: ————————————————

———————————————————————

Unusual traits: —————————————————

———————————————————————

Personality:————————————————————

———————————————————————

Tail type: ————————————————————
Ear type: ————————————————————
Comments: ————————————————————

———————————————————————

———————————————————————

———————————————————————

Date sighted: